Martina
the Beautiful Cockroach

The story of Martina the Cockroach and Perez the Mouse is one of the best known in Latin America, but there are also Persian, Indian, Spanish, and African variants of this tale. Carmen Agra Deedy's interpretation weaves some traditional motifs along with her own plot twists and childhood memories. Visit our website to learn more about Martina the Beautiful Cockroach at *www.beautifulmartina.com*

Published by
PEACHTREE PUBLISHERS
1700 Chattahoochee Avenue
Atlanta, Georgia 30318-2112
www.peachtree-online.com

Text © 2007 by Carmen Agra Deedy
Illustrations © 2007 by Michael Austin

First trade paperback edition published in 2014

Illustrations created in acrylic on Strathmore Series 500 illustration board. Titles created with Nick Curtis's Fontleroy Brown; text typeset in International Typeface Corporation's Belwe Light.

Printed in June 2016 by RR Donnelley & Sons in China
20 19 18 17 16 15 14 13 12 (hardcover)
10 9 8 7 6 5 4 (hardcover and CD package)
10 9 8 7 6 5 4 3 (trade paperback)

Library of Congress Cataloging-in-Publication Data

Deedy, Carmen Agra.
  Martina the beautiful cockroach : a Cuban folktale
/ retold by Carmen Agra Deedy ; illustrated by Michael Austin. — 1st ed.
    p. cm.
  Summary: In this humorous retelling of a Cuban folktale, a cockroach interviews her suitors in order to decide whom to marry.
  ISBN 978-1-56145-399-3 hardcover
  ISBN 978-1-56145-468-6 hardcover and CD package
  ISBN 978-1-56145-467-9 CD
  ISBN 978-1-56145-787-8 trade paperback
[1. Cockroaches—Folklore. 2. Folklore—Cuba.] I. Austin, Michael, 1965- ill. II. Title.
PZ8.1.D3782Mar 2007
398.2—dc22
[E]
                              2007003108

In memory of Abuela Graciela and Abuela Ofelia.

Thanks to my family, of course:
Papi and Mami; Katie, Erin, and Lauren;
Tersi, Ben, and Jordan.
And a special note of thanks to the children of
Holy Innocents' School and Davis Academy.

—C. A. D.

For Dad and Elisa

—M. A.

Martina
the Beautiful Cockroach

A CUBAN FOLKTALE

RETOLD BY
CARMEN AGRA DEEDY

ILLUSTRATED BY
MICHAEL AUSTIN

Ω
PEACHTREE
ATLANTA

Martina Josefina Catalina Cucaracha
was a beautiful cockroach.

She lived in a cozy
street lamp
in Old Havana
with her big, lovable family.

Now that Martina was 21 days old, she was ready to give
her leg in marriage. The Cucaracha household was crawling with
excitement! Every *señora* in the family had something to offer.

Tía Cuca gave her *una peineta*, a seashell comb.

Mamá gave her *una mantilla*, a lace shawl.

But *Abuela*, her Cuban grandmother, gave her
un consejo increíble, some shocking advice.

"You want me to do WHAT?" Martina was aghast.

"You are a beautiful cockroach," said *Abuela*. "Finding husbands to choose from will be easy—picking the right one could be tricky."

"B-b-but," stammered Martina, "how will spilling COFFEE on a suitor's shoes help me find a good husband?"

Her grandmother smiled. "It will make him angry! Then you'll know how he will speak to you when he loses his temper. Trust me, Martina. The Coffee Test never fails."

Martina wasn't so sure.

Meanwhile, *Papá* sent *el perico,* the parrot, to spread the word.

Soon all Havana—from the busy sidewalks of El Prado to El Morro castle—was abuzz with the news.

Martina the beautiful cockroach was ready to choose a husband.

As was the custom, Martina would greet

her suitors from the balcony, under her family's

many watchful eyes.

Daintily, she sat down

and crossed her legs,

and crossed her legs,

and crossed her legs.

She didn't have long to wait.

Don Gallo, the rooster, strutted up first. Martina tried not to stare at his splendid shoes.

Keeping one eye on his reflection, Don Gallo greeted her with a sweeping bow. "*¡Caramba!* You really are a beautiful cockroach. I will look even more fabulous with you on my wing!"

With that, he leaned forward and crooned,

"Martina
Josefina
Catalina
Cucaracha,
Beautiful *muchacha*,
Won't you be my wife?"

Martina hesitated only for an instant. "Coffee, *señor*?"

Right on cue, *Abuela* appeared.

With a quick glance at her grandmother, Martina nervously splattered coffee onto the rooster's spotless shoes.

"Oh my!" she said with mock dismay. "I'm all feelers today!"

"*¡Ki-ki-ri-kiiii!*" The rooster was furious. "Clumsy cockroach! I will teach you better manners when you are my wife."

Martina was stunned.
The Coffee Test had worked!
"A most humble offer, *señor*,"
she said cooly, "but I cannot
accept. You are much
too cocky for me."

Don Cerdo, the pig, hoofed up next. His smell curled the little hairs on Martina's legs.

"What an unimaginable scent," Martina wheezed. "Is it some new pig cologne?"

"Oh no, *señorita*. It's the sweet aroma of my pig sty. Rotten eggs! Turnip peels! Stinky cheese!" Don Cerdo licked his chops and sang,

"Martina
      Josefina
            Catalina
                  Cucaracha,
            Beautiful *muchacha*,
      Won't you be my wife?"

Martina had already left in search of coffee.

She wasted no time with the pig.

"*¡Gronc! ¡Gronc!*" squealed Don Cerdo
as he dabbed at the coffee on his shoes.
"What a tragedy for my poor loafers!"

He really is quite a ham,
thought Martina.

"Calm yourself, *señor.* I'll clean them for you!"

"I'll say you will!" he snorted. "When you are
my wife, there'll be no end to cleaning up after me!"

Martina rolled her eyes in disbelief.

"A most charming offer, *señor,*"
she said drily, "but I must decline.
You are much too boorish for me."

The Coffee Test had saved her
from yet another unsuitable suitor.

The pig was scarcely out of sight when Don Lagarto
the lizard, crept over the railing. His oily fingers brushed
the little cockroach's lovely *mantilla*.

"You shouldn't sneak up on a lady like that!"

"I don't sneak. I creep," he said, circling Martina.

For some reason this fellow really bugged her. "I've had
enough of creeps for one day," said Martina. *"Adiós."*

"But I need you! Wait!" The lizard fell on one
scaly knee and warbled,

"Martina
Josefina
Catalina
Cucaracha,
Beautiful *muchacha*,
Won't you be my wife?"

Martina sighed. "Let me see if there's any coffee left."

This time she wasn't taking any chances. Martina returned with TWO cups for the lizard.

"*¡Psssst! ¡Psssst!*" he spat. Don Lagarto was livid. He changed colors three times before he finally found his true one. "And to think," he hissed. "I was going to eat—er—MARRY you!"

Martina stared at the lizard. You could have heard a breadcrumb drop.

"Food for thought, *señor*," Martina said icily, "but I must refuse. You are much too cold-blooded for me."

When her grandmother returned to collect
the day's coffee cups, Martina was still fuming.

"I'm going inside, *Abuela*."

"So soon?"

"*¡Si!* I'm afraid of whom I might meet next!"

Abuela drew Martina to the railing and pointed
to the garden below. "What about him?"

Martina looked down at the tiny brown mouse,
and her cockroach heart began to beat faster.

Ti-ki-tin, ti-ki-tan.

"Oh, *Abuela*, he's adorable. Where has he been?"

"Right here all along."

"What do I do?"

"Go talk to him...and just be yourself."

Martina handed *Abuela* her *peineta* and *mantilla*,
then scurried down to the garden. The mouse was waiting.

Ti-ki-tin, ti-ki-tan.

"*Hola*, hello." His voice was like warm honey. "My name is Pérez."

"*Hola*," she whispered shyly, "I'm Martina—"

"—the beautiful cockroach," he finished for her.

"You think I'm beautiful?"

The little mouse turned pink under his fur. "Well, my eyes
are rather weak, but I have excellent EARS. I know you are
strong and good, Martina Josefina Catalina Cucaracha."
Then he squinted sweetly. "*Who cares if you are beautiful?*"

TI-KI-TIN, TI-KI-TAN.

"Martina-a-a-a-a! Don't forget the coffee!"
It was *Abuela*.

No, thought Martina. No coffee for Pérez!

"Martina Josefina Catalina Cucaracha!"

"*Sí, Abuela.*" Martina knew better than to
argue with her Cuban grandmother.

With a heavy heart, she reached for the cup.

But Pérez got there first.
Quick as a mouse, he splashed
café cubano onto Martina's shoes.

Now the coffee was on the other foot.

Martina was too delighted
to be angry. At last, she'd found
her perfect match. But she had
to ask, "How did you know
about the Coffee Test?"

Pérez grinned. "Well, *mi amor*,
my love…

…I too have a Cuban grandmother."